Divine Union; The Love Story of Lord Vishnu and Maa Lakshmi

Mrigendra Bharti

Published by Sellbrochure Vymish Entertainment, 2024.

This is a work of fiction. Similarities to real people, places, or events are entirely coincidental.

DIVINE UNION; THE LOVE STORY OF LORD VISHNU AND MAA LAKSHMI

First edition. July 12, 2024.

Copyright © 2024 Mrigendra Bharti.

ISBN: 979-8227804563

Written by Mrigendra Bharti.

Table of Contents

Preface

Within the vast tapestry of Hindu mythology, few narratives resonate as deeply as the love story of Vishnu, the preserver, and Lakshmi, the goddess of fortune and prosperity. Their union transcends the realm of mere romance; it embodies the very essence of cosmic balance, unwavering devotion, and the transformative power of love.

This book, "Divine Union: The Love Story of Lord Vishnu and Maa Lakshmi," delves into the heart of this epic tale. It explores their journey, from their first meeting amidst the churning of the cosmic ocean to their enduring bond that safeguards the universe.

Through captivating narratives and rich descriptions, we witness the unwavering support they offer each other, the strength they derive from their unity, and the wisdom they impart on the celestial beings and mortals alike. Their love story becomes a beacon of hope, a testament to the power of love to overcome adversity and inspire acts of compassion and righteousness.

This book is not merely a mythological recount. It offers valuable lessons that transcend time and culture. We learn about the importance of fostering harmonious relationships, the strength found in unwavering devotion, and the transformative power of love that binds not just individuals but also the very fabric of existence.

Whether you are a devout follower of Hinduism, a seeker of timeless love stories, or simply curious about the rich tapestry of mythology, "Divine Union" offers a captivating journey. Prepare to be swept away by the timeless tale of Vishnu and Lakshmi, a testament to the enduring power of love that shapes the cosmos itself.

Prologue

In the heart of an ageless expanse, where galaxies swirled like celestial dust and stars flickered like eternal flames, a faint echo resonated. It was a whisper from a time before time, a memory adrift in the cosmic ocean.

This echo carried a fragment of a story – a story of love woven into the very fabric of existence. It spoke of two divine beings, their spirits intertwined like the threads of fate. One, a figure of unwavering strength and serenity, the other radiating grace and compassion. Though details remained fragmented, the essence of their bond shone through – a love that defied definition, a love that transcended the boundaries of time and space.

As eons stretched on, this echo traversed the vastness of the cosmos, a testament to a love story that had shaped countless kalpas (cosmic ages). It brushed against nascent galaxies, whispered amongst the celestial bodies, and lingered in the hearts of countless beings.

Within the mortal realms, the echo manifested in countless ways. It bloomed in the unwavering devotion of lovers, the unwavering support of families, and the unwavering commitment to righteousness that flickered within the human spirit. It was a reminder, a whisper from across the ages, that the universe itself was born from and sustained by a love story of unparalleled power.

But the echo held another purpose. It served as a bridge, a connection between the kalpas, ensuring that the legacy of this epic love story wouldn't be lost. For within the grand cycle of creation, destruction, and recreation, a new chapter was about to unfold. A new kalpa was stirring, and with it, the need for a new avatar of Vishnu, the preserver.

And as the first tendrils of creation reached out into the cosmic void, the echo grew stronger, a beacon guiding the nascent consciousness of the new avatar. It was a call, a reminder of the purpose that awaited him, a legacy to uphold, and a love story to carry forward as the universe itself unfolded once more.

Acknowledgment

With a heart filled with humility and reverence, I bow my head in acknowledgement of the divine presence of Lord Vishnu and Goddess Lakshmi. As I present to you this humble offering, a book that delves into the depths of their extraordinary love story, I seek your forgiveness for any shortcomings or inaccuracies that may have inadvertently crept into its pages.

Throughout this journey of exploration, I have strived to capture the essence of their divine union, to paint a tapestry of words that reflects the brilliance of their love and the profound impact it has had on the cosmos. However, I recognize that my human limitations may have resulted in imperfections, in instances where my understanding of their divine nature fell short.

For this, I offer my sincerest apologies. I humbly seek forgiveness from Lord Vishnu, whose unwavering presence as the preserver of the universe is a source of eternal inspiration. I also seek forgiveness from Goddess Lakshmi, whose embodiment of fortune, prosperity, and compassion illuminates the path towards enlightenment.

I acknowledge that my use of simplified names, referring to Lord Vishnu as "Vishnu" and Goddess Lakshmi as "Lakshmi," may have caused unintended offense. This was never my intention, and I deeply regret any disrespect that may have arisen from this choice. My purpose was not to diminish their divine stature but rather to make their names more accessible to a wider audience.

I have learned that addressing divine beings with their full titles and epithets is a mark of utmost respect, and I pledge to adhere to this practice in the future. I will strive to represent their divine essence with the utmost reverence and accuracy in my future endeavors.

Finally, I extend my heartfelt gratitude to the readers who have embarked on this journey with me. Your willingness to engage with this story, to open your hearts to the power of their love, has been an immense source of encouragement.

With folded hands and a bowed head, I seek your forgiveness once again for any shortcomings in this work. May the blessings of Lord Vishnu and Goddess Lakshmi illuminate our paths and guide us towards a deeper understanding of their divine love.

WITH UTMOST HUMILITY,
    Mrigendra Bharti

About Sellbrochure Vymish Entertainment

Sellbrochure Vymish Entertainment, recognized as India's largest book publishing company, has made significant strides in ensuring its extensive collection of books reaches audiences across the global market. This rapid expansion is a testament to the company's dedication to disseminating knowledge and literature far beyond national borders. Central to its success is its affiliation with InkWhirl Media Networks, a reputable entity in the media and publication industry known for its innovative and strategic approaches. Within this network, InkWhirl Publication LLC operates as a vital division, further enhancing the company's capabilities and reach in the international market.

The visionary behind this enterprise is Mrigendra Bharti, the founder of Sellbrochure Vymish Entertainment. His foresight and passion for the literary world have been instrumental in steering the company towards remarkable growth and recognition. Under his leadership, Sellbrochure Vymish Entertainment has not only expanded its catalog but also established a strong presence in both domestic and international markets. Mrigendra Bharti's commitment to excellence and innovation has been a driving force in the company's journey, ensuring that it stays ahead of industry trends and meets the evolving needs of readers worldwide.

Sellbrochure Vymish Entertainment operates under the robust support of its parental organization, Mrigendra Bharti Group InfoTech. This affiliation provides the necessary resources and strategic guidance, enabling the publishing company to undertake ambitious projects and explore new markets. Mrigendra Bharti Group InfoTech's extensive experience in technology and information services has been a valuable asset, allowing Sellbrochure Vymish Entertainment to integrate advanced digital solutions in its operations, thereby enhancing its distribution capabilities and reader engagement.

Through relentless efforts and a commitment to quality, Sellbrochure Vymish Entertainment continues to break barriers and expand the reach of Indian literature globally. The company's diverse portfolio includes a wide range of genres, catering to different age groups and interests, thereby fostering a rich and inclusive reading culture. As it continues to innovate and grow, Sellbrochure Vymish Entertainment remains dedicated to its mission of making literature accessible to all, contributing significantly to the global literary landscape.

Connect With Mrigendra,
Thank you very much for choosing this book.
You can also connect with me on Instagram,
https://www.instagram.com/i_mrigendrabharti.official
With Love,
Mrigendra Bharti

Introduction

Welcome, dear reader, to a journey that transcends the boundaries of time and space. We embark on a voyage into the heart of Hindu mythology, where the very fabric of existence is woven with the threads of an epic love story – the love story of Vishnu, the preserver, and Lakshmi, the embodiment of fortune and prosperity.

Their union is more than just a celestial romance; it's a cosmic dance that embodies balance, devotion, and the transformative power of love. It's a story whispered across eons, a beacon of hope that inspires not just celestial beings but also mortals like ourselves.

Within these pages, you'll encounter captivating narratives that delve into the heart of their timeless bond. We'll witness their first meeting amidst the churning of the cosmic ocean, a pivotal moment that set the stage for their enduring connection. We'll explore the challenges they face, the unwavering support they offer each other, and the wisdom they impart on beings throughout the cosmos.

But this book is more than just a mythological recount. It's a treasure trove of timeless lessons that resonate across cultures and eras. We'll delve into the importance of fostering harmonious relationships, the strength found in unwavering devotion, and the transformative power of love that binds not just individuals but the very fabric of existence.

Whether you're a devout follower of Hinduism, a seeker of timeless love stories, or simply curious about the vast tapestry of mythology, "Divine Union" offers a captivating journey. Prepare to be swept away by the timeless tale of Vishnu and Lakshmi, a testament to the enduring power of love that shapes the very essence of the cosmos itself.

As you turn the pages, allow yourself to be transported to a celestial realm where love reigns supreme. Let the echoes of their love story resonate within you, reminding you of the power of love's embrace in our own lives.

So, dear reader, are you ready to embark on this extraordinary journey? Open your heart and mind, and let the divine union of Vishnu and Lakshmi unfold before you.

Chapter 1: The Churning of the Ocean

In the vast expanse of the cosmos, where stars twinkled like celestial diamonds and galaxies swirled in an eternal dance, a subtle imbalance had begun to manifest. The universe, once a harmonious symphony of creation, preservation, and destruction, was experiencing a gradual decline in its vibrancy. The nectar of immortality, Amrit, which sustained the gods and maintained the cosmic order, had been lost during the Great Deluge, leaving the universe vulnerable to decay and entropy.

Lord Vishnu, the preserver of the universe, recognized this growing imbalance and knew that drastic action was required. He sought counsel from his consort, Goddess Lakshmi, the embodiment of prosperity and abundance, whose wisdom was as vast as the cosmos itself. Together, they devised a plan to restore the universe's equilibrium – the churning of the ocean, a grand cosmic event that would yield Amrit, the elixir of life.

The churning of the ocean was not merely a physical undertaking; it was a symbolic representation of the universe's cyclical nature, a testament to the delicate balance between creation and destruction. It was a moment of immense power, where the very fabric of reality would be tested, and the fate of the universe would hang in the balance.

Lord Vishnu, ever the embodiment of strength and determination, assumed the form of Kurma, the colossal tortoise. His massive back, as broad as an island, would serve as the churning rod, providing the stability and foundation for this momentous endeavor.

The task of churning the ocean fell upon the mighty Vasuki serpent, whose serpentine form stretched for hundreds of miles. Coiling around Mount Mandara, a towering mountain that had been uprooted and cast into the ocean, Vasuki would serve as the churning rope, his powerful muscles propelling the mountain through the churning seas.

To provide the counterbalance, the gods and demons, once bitter rivals, were forced to unite for the sake of the universe's survival. The gods, led by Indra, the king of heaven, gripped the tail of Vasuki, their divine strength adding momentum to the churning. The demons, led by Bali, the mighty asura king, held the head of Vasuki, their combined power ensuring the churning was both powerful and controlled.

As the churning commenced, the ocean churned with such intensity that it transformed into a frothy whirlpool, its currents swirling with unimaginable force. Celestial beings watched in awe and anticipation as the churning continued, their hearts filled with a mixture of hope and trepidation.

From the depths of the churning ocean, a myriad of wondrous and unexpected treasures emerged. The first to appear was Halahala, a deadly poison that threatened to consume all life. Lord Shiva, the destroyer, stepped forward, swallowing the poison, his throat turning blue to contain its toxic power.

Next emerged the Kalpavriksha, the wish-granting tree, its branches laden with fruits and flowers that could fulfill any desire. The gods and demons eagerly claimed its branches, hoping to fulfill their long-held wishes.

From the churning also emerged Dhanvantari, the god of medicine, carrying with him the Amrit, the nectar of immortality. The gods rejoiced, their hearts filled with relief and hope. However, the demons, driven by greed and lust for power, snatched the Amrit from Dhanvantari, intending to consume it themselves and attain immortality.

Lord Vishnu, witnessing the demons' treachery, knew that he had to intervene. He assumed the form of Mohini, the enchanting enchantress, whose beauty and charm were unparalleled. The demons, captivated by Mohini's mesmerizing allure, surrendered the Amrit, unaware of her true identity.

Vishnu, having reclaimed the Amrit, distributed it among the gods, ensuring their immortality and restoring balance to the universe. The demons, once again defeated, were left to face the consequences of their greed and deceit.

The churning of the ocean had served its purpose, restoring the universe's equilibrium and reaffirming the power of unity and cooperation in the face of adversity. Lord Vishnu, Goddess Lakshmi, and the other celestial beings rejoiced, their hearts filled with gratitude for the restoration of cosmic harmony.

As the sun began to rise, casting its golden rays upon the tranquil ocean, the churning ceased, leaving behind a transformed world, one that was once again vibrant, balanced, and brimming with the promise of eternal life. The gods and demons, their rivalry temporarily set aside, returned to their respective realms, each carrying with them the lessons learned from this momentous event.

And so, the story of the churning of the ocean became an enduring legend, a testament to the power of love, unity, and the unwavering commitment to preserving the delicate balance of the cosmos.

The churning of the ocean was a spectacle of unimaginable power and chaos. Yet, amidst the churning seas and the tumultuous clash of celestial beings, an image of stoic resilience emerged – Lord Vishnu in his Kurma avatar. His colossal form, a magnificent blend of tortoise and deity, anchored the churning operation, providing the unwavering foundation upon which the fate of the universe rested.

Vishnu's transformation into Kurma was not merely a display of physical strength. It was a symbolic embodiment of his role as the preserver, the unwavering force that upholds the cosmic order. His immense shell, depicted as vast and indestructible, represented the shield that protects the universe from the relentless forces of destruction.

As the churning raged on, Kurma endured immense pressure. The churning ocean, a swirling vortex of celestial energy, threatened to topple him from his position. Yet, Kurma remained unfazed. His deep connection to the earth, symbolized by his tortoise form, provided him with unwavering stability. He bore the weight of Mount Mandara, the churning rod, and the immense counterbalancing forces of the gods and demons on his back with unwavering resolve.

His posture radiated a sense of calm amidst the chaos. His gaze, serene and focused, reflected his unwavering determination to see the churning through to its successful completion. His presence instilled a sense of reassurance in the celestial beings engaged in the churning. They knew that as long as Kurma remained steadfast, the universe would not succumb to the churning's destructive potential.

The act of Kurma bearing the weight of the world held a deeper significance. It mirrored the burden of responsibility that Vishnu carries as the preserver. He is the silent guardian, the unwavering force that ensures the universe continues to exist amidst the constant cycle of creation and destruction.

Kurma's sacrifice was not without its challenges. The churning process generated immense heat, threatening to scorch his shell. He endured the searing pain with stoic resolve, his focus unwavering from his task. Additionally, the churning produced a variety of toxins and poisons as different elements clashed within the ocean's depths. Yet, Kurma remained unaffected, his divine essence acting as a shield against these harmful substances.

Despite the immense challenges, Kurma's unwavering resolve never faltered. He embodied the qualities of patience, perseverance, and unwavering commitment, all essential aspects of the preserver. His form served as a constant reminder to the celestial beings, and by extension, to all living beings, that true strength lies not just in physical power but also in unwavering dedication to a greater purpose.

As the churning continued, a sense of awe and admiration grew among the celestial beings witnessing Kurma's unwavering resolve. He became a symbol of hope, a testament to the fact that even in the face of seemingly insurmountable challenges, unwavering commitment and unwavering purpose can ensure success. His sacrifice, his embodiment of the preserver, became an integral part of the legend of the churning of the ocean, a story that would forever be etched in the annals of cosmic history.

AS THE CHURNING OF the ocean intensified, a tremor of anticipation ran through the celestial beings gathered around the churning vortex. The churning had yielded various wonders - the wish-granting Kalpavriksha, the celestial cow Surabhi, and even the fearsome poison Halahala. But the most awaited treasure, the Amrit, the elixir of immortality, remained elusive.

Suddenly, a hush fell over the celestial assembly. The churning seas parted, and a radiant light erupted from the depths, illuminating the heavens. From the churning emerged a lotus flower, its pristine white petals unfurling gracefully. A gasp of awe escaped the celestial lips as a breathtaking vision unfolded before them. Seated majestically on the lotus, adorned with celestial jewels and draped in shimmering silk, was a woman of unparalleled beauty. Her dark eyes shone with wisdom and kindness, and her smile radiated warmth and compassion. It was Lakshmi, the embodiment of prosperity, abundance, and good fortune.

Lakshmi's emergence was more than just a spectacle; it was a sign of auspiciousness. Her very presence seemed to calm the churning seas, replacing the chaos with an aura of serenity. The celestial beings bowed in reverence, recognizing her as the divine consort of Lord Vishnu and the very essence of prosperity that the churning aimed to restore to the universe.

Lakshmi's arrival marked a turning point in the churning. Her presence served as a reminder that the churning was not just about obtaining the Amrit; it was about restoring balance and harmony to the cosmos. With Lakshmi's blessings, the churning process gained renewed vigor. The gods and demons, inspired by her divine presence, toiled with newfound determination, their rivalry temporarily forgotten in the face of this collective endeavor.

Lakshmi's beauty was not merely physical; it was an embodiment of divine qualities. Her grace and elegance personified prosperity, not just in terms of material wealth, but also in terms of spiritual abundance, good fortune, and well-being. Her presence instilled hope in the hearts of the celestial beings, reminding them that even amidst the chaos, there was the promise of a brighter future.

As Lakshmi surveyed the scene, her gaze fell upon Lord Vishnu, who stood resolute in his Kurma avatar, bearing the immense weight of Mount Mandara. A silent exchange passed between them, a communication that transcended words. It was a recognition of their shared purpose, a testament to their unwavering devotion to upholding the cosmic order.

Lakshmi's emergence from the ocean also held a deeper symbolic meaning. It represented the inherent connection between prosperity and preservation. True prosperity, Lakshmi embodied, could only flourish in a universe protected by the unwavering resolve of Vishnu, the preserver. Their combined presence signified the delicate balance between material and spiritual well-being, a balance essential for the sustenance of the cosmos.

The arrival of Lakshmi marked a shift in the narrative of the churning of the ocean. It was a moment of hope, a reminder that even in the midst of chaos, there is beauty, there is grace, and there is the promise of a brighter future. Her presence served as a beacon of light, guiding the celestial beings towards the successful completion of their task and the restoration of balance to the universe.

The emergence of Lakshmi from the churning ocean sent a ripple of awe and wonder through the celestial assembly. As the celestial beings bowed in reverence, a sense of hope blossomed in their hearts. Here, amidst the chaos and turmoil, stood the embodiment of prosperity and auspiciousness, a radiant beacon guiding them towards the restoration of cosmic equilibrium.

Lord Vishnu, steadfast in his Kurma avatar, acknowledged Lakshmi's arrival with a subtle shift in his gaze. A silent communication passed between them, a language woven from shared purpose and unwavering devotion. It was a testament to their divine bond, a union that symbolized the harmonious balance between preservation and prosperity, essential for the universe's well-being.

The churning continued with renewed vigor. Inspired by Lakshmi's divine presence, the gods and demons toiled with newfound determination, their rivalry temporarily set aside for the sake of the greater good. Lakshmi, adorned in celestial jewels and draped in shimmering silk, observed the scene with a gentle smile. Her presence instilled a sense of serenity, calming the churning seas and replacing the chaos with an aura of tranquility.

As the churning raged on, an undeniable spark ignited between Vishnu and Lakshmi. Vishnu, captivated by Lakshmi's radiant beauty and the divine aura that enveloped her, was awestruck. Her grace and elegance personified not just material wealth but also the essence of spiritual abundance, good fortune, and well-being. In her, he saw the embodiment of the very essence he sought to preserve – a universe brimming with prosperity and harmony.

Lakshmi, in turn, was deeply moved by Vishnu's unwavering resolve and dedication. His strength and determination, manifested in his Kurma avatar, resonated with her. She recognized in him the protector, the preserver who ensured the stability upon which true prosperity could flourish. Their gazes met, a silent conversation unfolding between them, a recognition of a bond destined to be.

Following the churning, as the celestial beings celebrated the retrieval of the Amrit, a sense of anticipation hung in the air. All eyes turned towards Vishnu and Lakshmi, their connection undeniable. With a gentle smile, Vishnu approached Lakshmi, his voice resonating with warmth and respect. He spoke of his admiration for her divine qualities, her embodiment of prosperity, and the hope she brought to the universe.

Lakshmi, her voice melodious and filled with grace, reciprocated his feelings. She acknowledged his role as the preserver, the protector upon whose unwavering shoulders rested the well-being of the cosmos. In him, she saw the perfect complement, the embodiment of stability that allowed prosperity to flourish.

And so, amidst the joyous celebration of the Amrit's retrieval, Vishnu and Lakshmi, two divine beings united by purpose and love, pledged their eternal devotion to each other. Their union symbolized the harmonious balance between preservation and prosperity, a cornerstone for the universe's continued existence. Their love story, whispered amongst the stars, became an enduring legend, a testament to the power of unity and the divine connection that binds the preserver and the embodiment of prosperity.

The churning of the ocean had not just yielded the Amrit; it had brought together two divine forces, their union a beacon of hope for a universe forever bound by the delicate balance of preservation and prosperity.

Chapter 2: The Celestial Abode: Vaikuntha

Beyond the celestial expanse, veiled by shimmering stardust, lay Vaikuntha, the magnificent abode of Lord Vishnu and his newlywed consort, Lakshmi. Unlike the vibrant chaos of the churning, Vaikuntha embodied tranquility and serenity. Here, celestial rivers flowed with the nectar of peace, and ethereal trees bore fruits that granted wishes and fulfilled desires.

Imagine a landscape painted with the soft hues of dawn. Lush meadows, carpeted with flowers of unimaginable colors, stretched as far as the eye could see. Gentle waterfalls cascaded down mountains sculpted from pure crystal, their melodies a constant symphony that soothed the soul. The air itself vibrated with a divine energy, invigorating and uplifting.

At the heart of Vaikuntha stood the celestial palace of Lord Vishnu and Lakshmi. Constructed from luminescent pearls and adorned with sapphires the size of planets, it shimmered with an otherworldly beauty. Celestial architects, the Vishwakarmas, had poured their artistry into its creation, weaving tales of the cosmos onto its walls and crafting ceilings that mirrored the starry expanse above.

The very essence of Vaikuntha embodied the divine qualities of Vishnu and Lakshmi. Tranquility, a reflection of Vishnu's preserving nature, permeated every corner. Prosperity, Lakshmi's domain, manifested in the abundance of celestial flora and fauna. Here, sorrow and suffering were banished, replaced by an eternal spring of serenity and joy.

Vaikuntha was not merely a beautiful abode; it was a refuge for the righteous, a haven for those seeking solace and liberation. Celestial beings, graced with the privilege of residing in Vaikuntha, spent their days in pious pursuits – chanting hymns in praise of the divine couple, meditating under celestial trees, and engaging in discourses on the nature of reality.

The arrival of Vishnu and Lakshmi marked a new era for Vaikuntha. Their presence further amplified the realm's radiance, casting a warm glow upon everything they touched. The celestial inhabitants rejoiced, their hearts swelling with devotion for the divine couple who had restored balance to the universe.

As you embark on this chapter, prepare to be enveloped by the serenity of Vaikuntha. Imagine the gentle caress of celestial winds, the soul-stirring melodies of the waterfalls, and the ever-present aura of peace that defines this extraordinary realm.

WITHIN THE CELESTIAL expanse of Vaikuntha, the palace of Lord Vishnu and Lakshmi stood as a testament to their divine union. Named Ananta, meaning "endless," the palace embodied the boundless nature of their love and the eternal realm they presided over. Unlike any earthly structure, Ananta defied architectural norms, its design a harmonious blend of grandeur and serenity.

The entrance to Ananta was guarded by gigantic celestial elephants, their ivory tusks gleaming like polished moons. As one passed through the colossal gates, a breathtaking vista unfolded. Crystal clear lakes reflected the luminescent glow of the palace, their surface dotted with celestial lotuses in perpetual bloom. Celestial swans, their feathers shimmering with iridescent hues, glided gracefully across the water, their calls adding to the symphony of tranquility.

The palace itself was a marvel of celestial craftsmanship. Its towering walls were constructed from shimmering pearls that cast a soft, ethereal glow. The Vishwakarmas, the divine architects, had meticulously carved scenes from the cosmos onto the pearl surface, depicting stories of creation, preservation, and destruction in exquisite detail. These celestial murals served as a constant reminder of the vastness of the universe and the divine couple's role in maintaining its balance.

As one ventured further into the palace, the air grew fragrant with the aroma of celestial flowers – mandara, parijata, and kalpavriksha blooms – their fragrance said to possess otherworldly properties that soothed the mind and uplifted the spirit. The floors were paved with sapphires, their smooth surfaces polished to a mirror-like sheen, reflecting the celestial brilliance that permeated every corner.

Within the palace, grand halls adorned with gold and studded with precious gems served as venues for celestial gatherings. Here, celestial beings would gather to sing hymns in praise of Vishnu and Lakshmi, their melodious voices echoing through the halls, creating a divine symphony that resonated throughout Vaikuntha.

Private chambers, each a masterpiece of artistry, provided havens for the divine couple. Vishnu's chamber, adorned with the blue hues of the cosmos, reflected his tranquil nature. Lakshmi's chamber, on the other hand, shimmered with the warm glow of golden lotuses, symbolizing prosperity and abundance. Yet, despite their distinct aesthetics, the chambers were connected by a hidden passage, a testament to the deep bond shared by the divine couple.

Ananta was not merely a place of opulence; it was a living, breathing entity that pulsed with the divine energy of Vishnu and Lakshmi. The very stones whispered tales of creation, the celestial flowers bloomed with an otherworldly vibrancy, and the air itself vibrated with a sense of peace and serenity. It was a fitting abode for the divine couple, a reflection of their celestial majesty and the harmony they brought to the cosmos.

Vaikuntha's serenity wasn't a silent solitude. The celestial realm thrummed with a vibrant life, its residents forming a diverse and devoted court that served Lord Vishnu and Lakshmi. Unlike earthly courts filled with intrigue and power struggles, the celestial court of Vaikuntha embodied devotion, harmony, and the pursuit of a higher purpose.

At the heart of the court stood the Gandharvas, heavenly musicians. These celestial beings, blessed with otherworldly voices and unparalleled musical talent, filled Vaikuntha with their enchanting melodies. Their music wasn't mere entertainment; it was a form of divine worship, weaving hymns that praised the divine couple and resonated with the very essence of creation. The Gandharvas, led by the celestial musician Tumburu, performed in the grand halls of Ananta, their music reaching every corner of Vaikuntha, uplifting the spirits of all celestial beings.

Alongside the Gandharvas were the Apsaras, celestial nymphs known for their breathtaking beauty and captivating dance. Clad in shimmering garments woven from moonlight and adorned with celestial flowers, they performed graceful dances that mirrored the cosmic cycles – the birth and death of stars, the creation and destruction of worlds. Their dances weren't mere displays of beauty; they were symbolic representations of the universe's constant state of flux, a reminder of Vishnu's role as the preserver amidst the grand dance of creation and destruction.

The celestial court also included the Kinnaras, beings with the head of a human and the body of a horse. Renowned for their storytelling abilities, they captivated the celestial audience with tales of creation, tales of Vishnu's avatars, and the divine couple's enduring love story. Their narratives served as a form of education, reminding celestial beings of their place in the cosmos and the importance of upholding righteousness and devotion.

Among the celestial court were also the Yakshas, a race of benevolent demigods known for their wisdom and guardianship. They served as protectors of Vaikuntha, their vigilance ensuring the continued peace and tranquility of the realm. They were also guardians of knowledge, possessing ancient texts that chronicled the history of the cosmos and the divine couple's deeds.

The celestial court wasn't just a collection of beings with unique talents; they were a unified force, bound by their devotion to Vishnu and Lakshmi. Each served a distinct purpose, contributing to the overall harmony and well-being of Vaikuntha. Whether it was the music of the Gandharvas, the dance of the Apsaras, the stories of the Kinnaras, or the vigilance of the Yakshas, each element worked in concert to create a vibrant celestial community dedicated to serving the divine couple.

This sense of unity wasn't forced; it stemmed from the inherent devotion that flowed from Vishnu and Lakshmi. Their presence radiated a sense of peace and purpose, inspiring the celestial beings to fulfill their roles with utmost dedication. In their presence, the celestial court didn't operate as a servant to masters, but as a family united in their devotion to a higher cause – the preservation of the cosmic order.

The celestial court served as a microcosm of the universe itself, a tapestry woven from diverse beings, each contributing to the greater whole. It was a reflection of the balance that Vishnu and Lakshmi strived to maintain – a harmony between music and dance, wisdom and vigilance, beauty and knowledge. As long as this vibrant court thrived, so did Vaikuntha, a testament to the divine couple's power to unite and inspire.

Life within Vaikuntha wasn't a stagnant state of serenity; it was a vibrant tapestry woven from daily rituals, spiritual pursuits, and moments of joyous celebration. Unlike the fleeting pleasures of the mortal world, the experiences in Vaikuntha resonated with a deeper meaning, enriching the souls of the celestial inhabitants and strengthening their connection with the divine.

Each day in Vaikuntha began with the gentle strumming of celestial veenas and the soft chanting of hymns. The Gandharvas and celestial sages would gather at the banks of the celestial rivers, their melodies echoing through the serene landscape, invoking blessings upon the divine couple for the day ahead. Celestial beings, clad in garments woven from moonlight and adorned with fragrant flowers, would join the hymns, their voices rising in a harmonious chorus that filled the air with a palpable sense of devotion.

Following the morning prayers, the celestial court would engage in intellectual discourses. Gathered in the grand halls of Ananta, sages and celestial scholars would delve into the profound mysteries of the universe, debating the nature of reality, the significance of karma, and the cycles of creation and destruction. Vishnu, renowned for his wisdom, would often participate in these discourses, enlightening the celestial beings with his insights and furthering their understanding of the cosmic order.

The discussions wouldn't be purely philosophical; they would often translate into practical applications. The Yakshas, drawing upon the wisdom gleaned from the discourse, would refine their strategies for protecting Vaikuntha. The Gandharvas, inspired by the discussions on the cosmic cycles, would create new compositions that mirrored the harmony and dissonance of creation and destruction.

The afternoons were dedicated to leisure and artistic pursuits. The celestial beings would gather in the celestial gardens, their laughter echoing amidst the vibrant blooms. Some would engage in friendly games, their competitive spirit tempered by a sense of camaraderie. Others would spend their time composing poetry, painting scenes of celestial beauty, or sculpting intricate figures depicting tales of the divine couple.

As dusk approached, the celestial beings would gather once more, this time for a celebration of gratitude. Offerings of celestial fruits and flowers would be presented to Vishnu and Lakshmi, accompanied by heartfelt prayers of thanksgiving for their continued blessings. The Gandharvas would play their most enchanting melodies, the Apsaras would perform mesmerizing dances, and the Kinnaras would narrate captivating tales that further underscored the divine couple's benevolence.

The evenings in Vaikuntha were imbued with a magical serenity. Celestial beings would gather on the banks of the shimmering lakes, gazing up at the star-studded expanse above. The celestial lights, unlike their mortal counterparts, weren't mere distant points of luminescence; they were celestial beings themselves, twinkling and swirling in a cosmic dance of their own. This spectacle served as a constant reminder of the vastness of the universe and the divine couple's role in maintaining its balance.

Life within Vaikuntha wasn't a monotonous cycle of rituals and celebrations; it was a dynamic interplay between devotion, intellectual exploration, and artistic expression. It was a life dedicated to serving a higher purpose, a life where every action, every thought, resonated with a deeper meaning. The inhabitants of Vaikuntha didn't merely exist; they thrived, their souls enriched by the divine presence of Vishnu and Lakshmi, their lives a testament to the true meaning of celestial bliss.

Chapter 3: Blessings and Trials

Life in Vaikuntha unfolded in a timeless rhythm, each day a testament to the divine couple's power to foster peace and serenity. Yet, amidst the tranquility, a subtle yearning began to blossom in the hearts of Vishnu and Lakshmi. While their celestial abode brimmed with joy and devotion, a sense of incompleteness lingered, a yearning for a deeper expression of their love.

One day, as Vishnu and Lakshmi strolled through the celestial gardens, their eyes fell upon a young celestial couple, Gandharva Vishvavasu and Apsara Menaka. Their love story, a melody of shared laughter and stolen glances, mirrored the very essence of the divine couple's own bond. As Vishnu watched them, a thought bloomed in his mind – the desire to bestow a blessing upon them, a blessing that would further enrich their love and bring forth a new chapter in their existence.

Vishnu approached the celestial couple, his presence radiating warmth and benevolence. Vishvavasu and Menaka, overcome with awe, bowed low in reverence. Vishnu, with a gentle smile, addressed them and spoke of their pure love, a love that resonated with the harmony of Vaikuntha. He expressed his desire to grant them a boon, a blessing that would deepen their bond and bring forth new life into their celestial existence.

Vishvavasu and Menaka, their hearts brimming with gratitude, expressed their deepest respect and devotion to the divine couple. They readily accepted the blessing, their faces aglow with anticipation for the joy it would bring. With a soft touch of his divine hand, Vishnu bestowed upon them the boon of fertility, a gift that would allow them to experience the miracle of creation within the celestial realm.

News of the blessing spread like wildfire through Vaikuntha, filling the celestial court with joy. The prospect of a new life, a child born under the divine couple's blessings, brought a sense of excitement and anticipation to the otherwise serene realm. The Gandharvas and Apsaras, inspired by Vishvavasu and Menaka's blessed union, started to view marriage with renewed purpose, recognizing it as a path to deepen their love and potentially receive blessings from the divine couple.

The celestial artisans, the Vishwakarmas, began crafting a magnificent nursery within the palace grounds of Ananta. They envisioned a haven for the celestial child, a space adorned with the finest celestial materials, imbued with divine energy to nurture its growth and well-being. The celestial sages, meanwhile, began researching ancient texts, seeking knowledge on the proper upbringing of a celestial child, ensuring it would grow into a being worthy of residing in Vaikuntha.

The blessing bestowed upon Vishvavasu and Menaka did more than just grant them a child; it revitalized Vaikuntha with a sense of hope and anticipation for the future. It served as a reminder that even within the realm of eternal bliss, there was room for growth, for creation, and for the blossoming of new life blessed by the divine couple. The celestial court eagerly awaited the arrival of this child, a symbol of the divine couple's benevolence and a testament to the enduring power of love.

The celestial realm buzzed with anticipation as the days turned into weeks, and weeks into months. Vishvavasu and Menaka, blessed by Vishnu and Lakshmi, experienced the transformative power of creation within them. Their love, already a source of joy in Vaikuntha, blossomed with a deeper purpose, a shared excitement for the life growing within Menaka.

The celestial artisans, the Vishwakarmas, completed their work on the wondrous nursery. Crafted from moonstone and adorned with celestial flowers that bloomed with the colors of the dawn, it was a space of unparalleled beauty and tranquility. The celestial sages, having delved into ancient texts, devised a curriculum for the child's upbringing, one that would nurture its divine potential alongside its celestial virtues.

Finally, the day of birth arrived. A hush fell over Vaikuntha as celestial beings gathered outside the nursery, their eyes filled with anticipation. Menaka, bathed in the soft glow of celestial light, experienced the miracle of childbirth – a process imbued with divine energy and a sense of serenity unlike anything experienced in the mortal realm.

As the first cries of the newborn echoed through the halls of Ananta, a wave of joy swept through Vaikuntha. Vishnu and Lakshmi, their faces beaming with a divine light, entered the nursery to witness the arrival of the celestial child. There, nestled amidst the celestial blooms, lay a radiant being, his tiny form radiating an ethereal glow.

The celestial sages, drawing upon their knowledge, named the child Kamadeva, meaning "the god of love." His arrival was more than just a birth; it was a momentous occasion, the first creation within Vaikuntha since its inception. Kamadeva embodied the essence of love – the very force that had bound Vishnu and Lakshmi together and that resonated throughout the celestial realm.

As Kamadeva grew, his presence brought a unique energy to Vaikuntha. His laughter, like the tinkling of celestial bells, filled the air with a newfound joy. His playful antics, a reflection of his youthful innocence, brought smiles to the faces of even the most stoic celestial beings. He forged an effortless connection with everyone, his charm acting as a bridge between the different celestial races – Gandharvas, Apsaras, Kinnaras, and Yakshas.

However, with the joy of Kamadeva's presence came an unforeseen consequence. His very essence – love – began to stir a dormant yearning within the hearts of the celestial beings. They started to yearn for experiences beyond the serene routine of Vaikuntha, for a deeper connection that mirrored the love shared by Vishvavasu and Menaka.

This yearning, while seemingly innocent, presented a potential threat to the tranquility of Vaikuntha. The pursuit of passionate love, unlike the devoted love that permeated the realm, could lead to jealousy, rivalry, and discord. The celestial court, once a harmonious unit, faced the possibility of fracturing under the influence of newfound desires.

Vishnu and Lakshmi recognized the potential danger. While they rejoiced in the joy and love that Kamadeva brought, they also understood the need to safeguard the peace of Vaikuntha. They realized that Kamadeva, in his youthful innocence, needed guidance to ensure his power of love wouldn't disrupt the delicate balance of the celestial realm. A challenge loomed – to ensure Kamadeva's divine potential flourished while protecting Vaikuntha from the unforeseen consequences of unleashed passion.

The prospect of Kamadeva's burgeoning power disrupting the tranquility of Vaikuntha presented a unique challenge for Vishnu and Lakshmi. Unlike the external threats they had faced in the past, this issue stemmed from within, a consequence of the very love they had blessed. To address this challenge, they opted for a solution that embodied both wisdom and subtlety.

Vishnu, known for his cunning and ability to maintain cosmic balance, decided to take on the role of Kamadeva's mentor. He envisioned channeling Kamadeva's potent energy towards a more refined form of love – a love that fostered devotion, compassion, and a deeper understanding of the divine order.

Vishnu approached Kamadeva not with stern pronouncements or restrictions, but with playful curiosity. He would engage Kamadeva in games and competitions, testing his skills and agility. Through these playful interactions, Vishnu subtly imparted valuable lessons. He taught him about the power of archery, not to spark fiery passions, but to wield love as a force for good, uniting hearts in harmonious bonds.

Lakshmi, the embodiment of grace and refinement, took a different approach. She would spend time with Kamadeva, teaching him the art of dance, storytelling, and poetry. Through these artistic pursuits, she instilled in him the power of love to inspire beauty, creativity, and a deeper appreciation for the divine essence that permeated Vaikuntha.

Vishnu and Lakshmi's combined efforts bore fruit. Kamadeva, under their patient guidance, began to comprehend the true nature of love. He realized that love wasn't just about fleeting desires, but about fostering a deeper connection – a connection that resonated with the divine harmony of Vaikuntha. His arrows, once envisioned as weapons of desire, transformed into symbols of devotion, forging bonds built on respect and understanding.

The celestial court, witnessing Kamadeva's transformation, felt their own yearnings shift. The passionate desires they had initially felt began to morph into a more refined sentiment. They started to appreciate the love that already existed in Vaikuntha – the love between spouses, the love between friends, the love for their celestial abode, and most importantly, the love for the divine couple who presided over their realm.

The potential conflict was averted. Kamadeva, no longer a harbinger of discord, became a symbol of the refined and transformative power of love. He continued to play with the celestial beings, his games and stories no longer stirring up unrest but fostering a sense of camaraderie and joy. He became a bridge between the different races, his playful spirit uniting them under the common banner of celestial love.

The challenge of Kamadeva's birth served as a valuable lesson for Vishnu and Lakshmi. It reminded them that even within the seemingly unchanging serenity of Vaikuntha, change and adaptation were essential. By guiding Kamadeva's growth, they ensured that the powerful force of love would not disrupt the balance they strived to maintain.

Vaikuntha continued to thrive, but now with a newfound appreciation for the multifaceted nature of love. The celestial beings, inspired by the divine couple and the lessons learned from Kamadeva, carried the torch of refined love, ensuring that their celestial abode remained a haven of peace, devotion, and a testament to the enduring power of the divine couple who presided over it.

The tranquility of Vaikuntha wasn't destined to last forever. Whispers of unrest began to permeate the celestial realm, originating from beyond its shimmering borders. News traveled through celestial messengers, tales of a growing imbalance in the mortal world. Greed, hatred, and violence were on the rise, disrupting the delicate harmony that Vishnu, as the Preserver, sought to maintain.

The source of this turmoil was a powerful demon king named Tarakasura. He had risen to power through deceit and cruelty, his reign of terror plunging the mortal world into chaos. Tarakasura, blinded by ambition, yearned for immortality, a desire that threatened to disrupt the cosmic order.

The celestial sages, upon learning of Tarakasura's ambitions, consulted ancient prophecies. They discovered a passage foretelling that only a son born of the divine fire, Agni, and the river Ganga, could vanquish the demon king. However, a celestial child born from such powerful entities presented a challenge.

Agni, the god of fire, was known for his fierce temper and unpredictable nature. Ganga, the personification of the celestial river, embodied purity and serenity. Bringing these two contrasting forces together for the sole purpose of creating a warrior was a task fraught with difficulty.

News of the prophecy reached Vaikuntha, casting a shadow over the usually joyous atmosphere. Vishnu and Lakshmi, recognizing the threat Tarakasura posed to the mortal world and the cosmic balance, knew they had to act. However, they understood the inherent dangers of manipulating divine forces for a singular purpose.

After much deliberation, Vishnu formulated a plan. He wouldn't force Agni and Ganga together; instead, he would create an environment where they would willingly unite for the greater good. He decided to take on a unique avatar, a form that embodied both Agni's fiery spirit and the calming essence of Ganga.

Vishnu donned the form of a captivating mendicant, his appearance radiating a paradoxical aura of both heat and serenity. He ventured out from Vaikuntha, his destination – the celestial abode of Agni, the god of fire.

Meanwhile, Lakshmi, aware of the emotional turmoil Agni and Ganga might experience, devised a plan of her own. She sent celestial messengers to Ganga, carrying gifts and messages of compassion, reminding her of her role as the nurturer and protector of life.

The arrival of Vishnu in his mendicant form caught Agni off guard. Intrigued by the divine visitor's enigmatic aura, Agni welcomed him into his fiery abode. Vishnu, with his serene demeanor and insightful words, engaged Agni in philosophical discussions. He spoke of the importance of balance, of tempering fiery passion with wisdom and compassion.

Ganga, upon receiving Lakshmi's gifts and messages, was touched by the reminder of her celestial duty. She saw the potential for destruction in Tarakasura's reign and recognized the responsibility that came with her divine power.

As Vishnu's discussions with Agni progressed, he subtly began to weave tales of Tarakasura's growing tyranny. He spoke of the suffering in the mortal world, the disruption of the cosmic order, and the need for a force of both strength and compassion to restore balance. Agni, his fiery spirit stirred by the tales of injustice, felt a spark of righteous anger ignite within him.

Meanwhile, Lakshmi continued to send messages to Ganga. She spoke of the potential for creation from the union of fire and water, of the birth of a champion who could bring an end to Tarakasura's reign and restore peace to the mortal world.

The seeds of action had been sown. Both Agni and Ganga, drawn by a sense of responsibility and a newfound understanding of the situation, felt a willingness to participate in a divine union. Vishnu, sensing their shift in perspective, knew the time was right.

He revealed his true form, his celestial radiance dispelling the fiery glow of Agni's abode. He spoke of his role as the Preserver, his desire to maintain order and protect the innocent. He then proposed a solution – a temporary union between Agni and Ganga, a union that could bring forth a champion capable of defeating Tarakasura and restoring balance to the cosmos.

Agni, his fiery spirit now tempered with a sense of purpose, readily agreed. Ganga, recognizing the potential for good, also accepted Vishnu's proposal. With a celestial blessing from Vishnu, Agni and Ganga entered into a temporary union, their contrasting energies merging for a brief yet momentous occasion.

From this union emerged a radiant being, a child born of fire and water – a testament to the power of unity and the wisdom of the divine couple. This child, destined to become a legendary warrior, would embark on a perilous journey to confront Tarakasura, a journey that would test his strength, his courage, and his understanding of the true meaning of being a champion.

The tranquility of Vaikuntha...had been disrupted, but not shattered. The news of the child's birth brought a renewed sense of hope to the celestial realm. Vishnu, his purpose fulfilled, returned to Vaikuntha alongside Lakshmi. The divine couple, though burdened by the coming conflict, found solace in the knowledge that they had taken a crucial step towards restoring balance.

Meanwhile, the celestial child, yet unnamed, was entrusted to the care of the celestial sages. They nurtured him, imparting knowledge of warfare, strategy, and the divine principles that underpinned the cosmic order. As the child grew, his abilities blossomed. He displayed the fiery spirit of Agni, his attacks swift and relentless. He also possessed the calming presence of Ganga, his movements precise and controlled. He was a formidable warrior in the making, a beacon of hope for the suffering mortals.

News of the child's exceptional abilities reached Tarakasura's ears. The demon king, initially skeptical, grew increasingly alarmed. He recognized the potential threat this celestial child posed to his reign. He dispatched his most fearsome demon warriors to capture the child before he reached his full potential.

However, the celestial sages, anticipating such a move, had prepared for this very moment. They devised a plan to transport the child to a hidden location within the mortal realm, a place shielded by powerful enchantments. This hidden haven would serve as the child's training ground, a place where he could hone his skills and prepare for the inevitable confrontation with Tarakasura.

The journey to the mortal realm was fraught with danger. The demon warriors, relentless in their pursuit, followed the faint celestial trail left behind. The child, shielded by the sages' magic, remained unaware of the danger. He spent his days exploring the wonders of the mortal world, his innocence a stark contrast to the turmoil brewing around him.

The celestial sages, acting as his mentors, began his training in earnest. They taught him not just the art of war, but also the importance of compassion, empathy, and understanding the plight of the mortals he was destined to protect. They instilled in him the values that would make him not just a powerful warrior, but a true champion for the forces of good.

As the child trained, honing his skills and growing into a young man, the news of his existence spread like wildfire amongst the mortals. Whispers of a divine champion destined to vanquish Tarakasura brought a glimmer of hope to the oppressed populace. They began to see him as a symbol of liberation, a force that could usher in an era of peace and prosperity.

The stage was set for a momentous clash. In the hidden haven within the mortal realm, a young warrior trained tirelessly, his celestial lineage and potent abilities making him a formidable adversary. In his distant abode, Tarakasura, consumed by paranoia and fear, prepared for the inevitable confrontation. The tranquility of Vaikuntha had been disrupted, but from it emerged a champion, a symbol of hope, destined to restore balance to the cosmos. The fate of the mortals, and the very fabric of reality, hung in the balance as the young warrior prepared to face the demon king.

Chapter 4: The Enduring Love

Vaikuntha reverberated with jubilation. The news of Vishnu and Lakshmi's triumph over the demon king echoed through the celestial abode, igniting a wave of euphoria. The celestial beings, for long burdened by the shadow of the demon's reign, emerged from their dwellings, their faces beaming with relief and gratitude. Grand preparations were underway for a celebration unlike any other - a testament to the divine couple's victory and a reaffirmation of their unwavering commitment to safeguarding the cosmos.

The celestial artisans, renowned for their mastery over ethereal materials, spared no effort in transforming Vaikuntha into a spectacle of unparalleled beauty. Strings of celestial pearls, imbued with the luminescence of a thousand moons, adorned the majestic trees of Kalpavriksha, their boughs laden with fruits that bestowed divine blessings. Celestial flowers, woven into intricate tapestries, adorned the pathways, their fragrance filling the air with an intoxicating sweetness. The celestial architects, wielding the power of divine geometry, constructed magnificent pavilions that shimmered with an otherworldly glow, their halls echoing with the celestial music played by the divine Gandharvas.

At the heart of this celestial spectacle stood the resplendent palace of Vishnu and Lakshmi. Its luminescence, emanating from precious jewels and enchanted stones, rivaled the brilliance of the celestial sun. Inside, the preparations were equally meticulous. Apsaras, clad in shimmering garments woven from moonlight, flitted about the grand hall, arranging celestial flowers and ensuring every detail was flawless. The air hummed with anticipation, a collective sigh of relief and joy permeating the atmosphere.

Finally, the moment of arrival dawned. A celestial chariot, drawn by magnificent swans with plumage that shimmered like molten gold, descended from the heavens. As it touched down on the celestial platform, a hush fell over the gathered multitude. The chariot doors creaked open, revealing the divine couple in all their resplendence.

Vishnu, his regal form draped in celestial attire woven from starlight, emanated an aura of serenity and power. A faint smile played on his lips, reflecting the joyous occasion. Lakshmi, a vision of unparalleled beauty, adorned with jewels that glittered like captured constellations, radiated warmth and grace. Her presence, like the gentle caress of a spring breeze, calmed the very air around her.

As they stepped out of the chariot, a collective gasp of awe rippled through the crowd. The celestial beings, overwhelmed by the divine aura of the couple, bowed their heads in reverence. Vishnu, his gaze filled with love and appreciation, offered his hand to Lakshmi. She took it gracefully, their fingers intertwining in a gesture of unity and love that had protected the cosmos for millennia.

The celestial musicians, their instruments echoing with newfound vigor, erupted into a symphony of celestial melodies. The Gandharvas sang hymns praising the divine couple's valor and their unwavering dedication to the preservation of harmony. A thousand celestial maidens, dressed in shimmering attire, twirled and swayed in a graceful dance, their movements mirroring the rhythm of the cosmos.

Vishnu and Lakshmi, hand in hand, walked amidst the jubilant crowd. They greeted their celestial kin, their smiles radiating warmth and acknowledging the sacrifices made during the dark times. They exchanged words of comfort with those who had lost loved ones during the demon's reign, their divine presence offering solace and a promise of a brighter future.

The celebration continued for a celestial fortnight, a testament to the enduring love and unwavering commitment of Vishnu and Lakshmi. It was a time for revelry, a time for renewal, and a time for the celestial beings to reaffirm their faith in the divine couple who stood as the guardians of the cosmos. As the festivities reached their crescendo, a sense of peace and harmony settled upon Vaikuntha, a stark contrast to the turmoil they had endured. The victory over the demon king was a significant milestone, but for Vishnu and Lakshmi, it was merely a chapter in their eternal saga, a saga that would forever bind their love to the fate of the universe.

The celebratory fervor that had swept through Vaikuntha gradually subsided, giving way to a sense of tranquil joy. The celestial beings returned to their duties, their hearts lighter and their spirits renewed by the recent victory. Yet, amidst the routine of celestial life, tender moments continued to unfold between Vishnu and Lakshmi, expressions of their love that transcended the grand pronouncements and celebrations.

One such moment dawned on a serene morning in Vaikuntha. The air shimmered with the soft glow of the celestial sun, casting long shadows from the Kalpavriksha trees. Vishnu, adorned in simple white attire, sat beneath a sprawling tree, his eyes closed in meditation. His brow was unfurrowed, a rare sight after the trials they had faced. Lakshmi, draped in a flowing blue silk saree, approached him silently. Her movements were graceful, her presence a gentle breeze rustling through the leaves.

As she neared him, Vishnu opened his eyes, a wave of warmth washing over his features. He gestured beside him, and Lakshmi settled down gracefully. They sat in comfortable silence, a language only they understood passing between them. It was a silence filled with unspoken emotions, a deep understanding forged through eons of shared experiences.

Suddenly, a playful glint sparked in Lakshmi's eyes. She plucked a fragrant blossom from a nearby plant and, with a mischievous smile, placed it behind Vishnu's ear. His eyes widened in mock surprise, and a chuckle escaped his lips. He turned to her, his gaze filled with affection.

"Always the playful one, my love," he said, his voice tinged with amusement.

"Someone needs to bring a smile to your face after all those battles and cosmic worries," Lakshmi replied, her voice a melodious chime.

They spent the next hour in conversation, their words flowing like a gentle stream. They reminisced about their journey together, from their first meeting amidst the churning ocean to the challenges they had faced as guardians of the cosmos. Lakshmi spoke of the fear she felt during the battles against demons, her voice trembling slightly. Vishnu, ever the source of comfort, reached for her hand, his touch a silent reassurance.

"We faced them together, my love," he said, his voice firm yet gentle. "And together, we will face whatever challenges may come our way."

Lakshmi nodded, her hand finding solace in his. They spoke of their hopes for the future, for a universe brimming with peace and prosperity. They discussed their plans to nurture the mortal realms, to guide them towards a brighter future. Their conversation wasn't just about grand pronouncements; it was about the intricate details that made up the tapestry of their love – the unwavering support, the shared dreams, and the quiet moments of vulnerability.

As the sun began its descent, casting an ethereal glow across Vaikuntha, Vishnu and Lakshmi rose from their place beneath the tree. Their faces, bathed in the golden light, reflected the contentment that filled their hearts. With a tender smile, Vishnu offered his arm to Lakshmi, and they walked hand-in-hand towards their palace, their love story a beacon of light in the vast expanse of the cosmos.

Later that evening, as the celestial palace shimmered with the soft glow of moonstones, Vishnu and Lakshmi sat on their balcony, gazing out at the star-studded expanse. The celestial city of Vaikuntha lay sprawled before them, a testament to the harmony they strived to maintain.

"The universe seems brighter tonight," Lakshmi remarked, her voice soft as a whisper.

"It is because of you, my love," Vishnu replied, his gaze fixed on her. "Your presence casts a light that illuminates even the darkest corners."

Lakshmi leaned her head against his shoulder, a gesture of silent affection. They sat in comfortable silence, the celestial landscape their only audience. In that moment, their love wasn't a grand spectacle; it was a quiet intimacy, a shared understanding that transcended words. It was in these quiet moments, away from the pomp and ceremony, that the true essence of their love shone the brightest – a love story woven into the fabric of the cosmos itself.

News of Vishnu and Lakshmi's unwavering love story resonated throughout the celestial realms. Their bond, a testament to devotion, compassion, and unwavering support, became a beacon of hope for countless beings. Among those inspired was Amruta, a young apsara renowned for her celestial music and unwavering devotion to the divine couple.

Amruta, unlike her carefree celestial kin, harbored a deep longing for a love that mirrored the one she witnessed between Vishnu and Lakshmi. However, her heart remained unclaimed. Though many celestial suitors sought her hand, none could ignite the spark she yearned for.

One day, overcome by her yearning, Amruta decided to seek the blessings of Vishnu and Lakshmi. She journeyed to Vaikuntha, her heart filled with a mixture of hope and trepidation. As she approached the celestial palace, its grandeur momentarily overwhelmed her. Yet, gathering her courage, she requested an audience with the divine couple.

Her request was granted, and Amruta found herself standing before Vishnu and Lakshmi, their divine presence filling the room with an aura of serenity. With a reverence bordering on awe, she bowed low, her voice trembling as she spoke.

"Esteemed Vishnu and Lakshmi," she began, "your love story has been the guiding light of my existence. It has shown me the true meaning of devotion, understanding, and the strength that love can provide."

Vishnu and Lakshmi exchanged a knowing glance, their eyes filled with compassion. They sensed the sincerity in Amruta's words and the genuine yearning in her heart.

Amruta continued, her voice gaining strength, "For years, I have longed for a love that reflects yours, a love built on mutual respect and unwavering support. Yet, such a love has eluded me."

A gentle smile played on Lakshmi's lips. "Love, dear Amruta," she said, her voice like a soothing melody, "is a journey, not a destination. It takes time, patience, and a willingness to open your heart to possibilities."

Vishnu added, his voice resonating with wisdom, "True love doesn't demand perfection; it embraces imperfections. It thrives on understanding and grows stronger with each shared experience."

Amruta listened intently, her heart absorbing their words like a parched land receiving rain. A sense of clarity began to dawn upon her. Perhaps, she realized, she had been searching for a love that mirrored a grand spectacle, neglecting the possibility of a love story unfolding in its own unique way.

Taking a deep breath, Amruta bowed her head once more. "Thank you, divine ones," she said, her voice filled with gratitude. "Your wisdom has illuminated my path."

Vishnu and Lakshmi offered her a reassuring smile. They knew her journey towards love had just begun, but they also recognized the newfound strength that blossomed within her.

As Amruta departed from Vaikuntha, a sense of hope filled her heart. The divine couple's blessing wasn't a promise of instant fulfillment; it was a gentle nudge in the right direction. They had instilled in her the importance of self-discovery, of recognizing the qualities she sought in a partner, and of remaining open to the possibilities that lay ahead.

Inspired by Vishnu and Lakshmi's love story, Amruta began to approach her celestial suitors with a newfound perspective.

She no longer sought a mirror image of their divine bond; instead, she searched for someone who complemented her own unique qualities, someone with whom she could build a love story based on mutual respect, understanding, and shared experiences.

Her journey wasn't without its challenges. There were moments of doubt, of yearning for a love that seemed elusive. But through it all, Amruta held onto the lessons she had learned from Vishnu and Lakshmi. She remained true to herself, her heart open to possibilities.

And then, one day, she met him. A young Gandharva, renowned for his celestial music, crossed her path. Their initial encounter was a spark, a shared passion for music igniting a connection. As they spent more time together, Amruta discovered a depth of understanding and respect that resonated within her. He saw her not just for her celestial beauty but for the strength and compassion that resided within her.

Their love story unfolded slowly, organically, like a gentle melody weaving its way through the celestial realms. It wasn't a grand spectacle; it was a testament to the transformative power of genuine connection, nurtured by the lessons learned from the enduring love of Vishnu and Lakshmi. Amruta's story became a testament to the ripple effect of their love, a beacon of hope, inspiring countless others to believe in the possibility of finding their own unique love stories within the vast tapestry of the cosmos.

Vishnu and Lakshmi's love story wasn't just a celestial spectacle; it was a timeless narrative woven into the very fabric of the cosmos. Their unwavering devotion, their unwavering support for each other, and their unwavering commitment to preserving harmony resonated with countless beings across the eons. They became an embodiment of the ideal love story, a testament to the power of love to overcome any obstacle and a source of inspiration for mortals and celestial beings alike.

Devotees across the mortal realms offered prayers and hymns to Vishnu and Lakshmi, seeking blessings for their own relationships. Temples dedicated to the divine couple became centers of pilgrimage, where devotees sought not just material prosperity but also the strength and understanding that characterized their love. Through these acts of devotion, a connection blossomed between the divine couple and their mortal followers.

Vishnu and Lakshmi, ever aware of the impact their love story had, actively nurtured this connection. They blessed countless couples seeking to embark on the journey of marriage, offering them guidance and support. They intervened in situations where love faltered, reminding couples of the importance of communication, compromise, and unwavering commitment. Their presence, even if unseen, served as a beacon of hope, reminding couples that even amidst challenges, love could endure and grow stronger.

One such instance involved a young couple named Maya and Arjun. Their love story, once vibrant, had become strained by misunderstandings and a lack of communication. As their arguments grew more frequent and their affection for one another dwindled, they contemplated separation.

Desperate to salvage their relationship, Maya embarked on a pilgrimage to a temple dedicated to Vishnu and Lakshmi. With a heart filled with longing and regret, she stood before their idols, offering a silent prayer. She poured out her heart, confessing her fears and anxieties about losing Arjun. As she prayed, a sense of calm washed over her. She realized that the love she shared with Arjun was worth fighting for.

Returning home, Maya approached Arjun with a newfound resolve. She confessed her feelings, expressing her desire to mend their broken bond. Arjun, moved by her sincerity and the strength he witnessed in her, reciprocated her feelings. Together, they sought guidance from a wise elder who instilled in them the importance of communication and empathy. They learned to listen to each other, to understand each other's perspectives, and to work through their differences with patience and love.

Slowly, their relationship began to heal. They rediscovered the joy of shared experiences, the comfort of mutual respect, and the strength that came from being a united front. Their love story, once on the brink of collapse, was revitalized by the blessings of Vishnu and Lakshmi, a testament to the transformative power of their enduring love.

The story of Maya and Arjun became a beacon of hope for countless others facing challenges in their relationships. It served as a reminder that even the strongest bonds can be tested, but with dedication, perseverance, and the inspiration drawn from the divine couple's love story, love could be rekindled, and relationships could be strengthened.

As the cosmos continued its endless cycle of creation, destruction, and recreation, Vishnu and Lakshmi's love story remained a constant. Even when the universe plunged into darkness during the Pralaya, the great dissolution, their love endured, a flickering ember waiting to ignite the spark of creation once more. Their avatars, born anew in each kalpa (cosmic age), carried their legacy forward, reminding mortals and celestials alike of the enduring power of love.

Vishnu and Lakshmi's love story wasn't just a timeless narrative; it was a living testament to the power of love in all its forms. It was a beacon of hope, a source of inspiration, and a reminder that even in the vast expanse of the cosmos, the most powerful force remained the unwavering love that bound two souls together.

Chapter 5: The Eternal Promise

The cosmos, an entity both majestic and enigmatic, existed in a perpetual state of flux. Eons stretched before the beginning, and eons would stretch beyond the end. This grand cosmic dance comprised an intricate cycle – creation (srishti), preservation (sthiti), and destruction (samhara). Vishnu, the preserver, played a pivotal role in this cycle, his avatars appearing in each kalpa (cosmic age) to restore balance and safeguard the universe from the forces of chaos.

The current kalpa had witnessed its fair share of upheaval. From the churning of the cosmic ocean to the recent triumph over the demon king, Vishnu, along with Lakshmi by his side, had ensured the continued existence of the universe. Yet, they were well aware that this was merely a chapter in the grand cosmic narrative. The cycle would continue, and the need for preservation would arise once more.

One evening, as they sat on their celestial balcony in Vaikuntha, gazing at the star-studded expanse, Vishnu turned to Lakshmi, his voice laced with a hint of melancholy.

"My love," he began, "as you know, the cycle knows no rest. Even now, the seeds of Pralaya, the great dissolution, are sown in the distant future."

Lakshmi offered him a gentle smile, her eyes filled with unwavering faith. "Indeed, my love," she replied. "But even in the face of destruction, our love will endure."

They both understood the inevitable. The universe, in its grand design, would eventually plunge into darkness, all existence dissolving into a primordial chaos. Yet, their love, a force that transcended the boundaries of time and space, would remain untouched. It was a cosmic constant, an ember that would flicker even in the face of oblivion.

Vishnu continued, his voice low and thoughtful, "My avatars, born anew in each kalpa, will continue their duty of restoring balance. But with each creation, the memories of the past kalpa fade."

This was a source of concern for him. He envisioned the challenges his future avatars might face, the battles against darkness they would have to fight without the knowledge gleaned from past victories.

Sensing his concern, Lakshmi placed a comforting hand on his arm. "Your wisdom and compassion will guide them, my love," she assured him. "The essence of your being, the principles of preservation and harmony you embody, will be carried forward within them."

Her words resonated with truth. Vishnu, the preserver, was more than just a physical form. He was an embodiment of cosmic principles, and these principles would transcend the limitations of time and space. Every avatar, no matter how different their appearance or circumstances, would carry within them the essence of Vishnu – the unwavering dedication to preserving harmony and upholding righteousness.

"But what of love?" Vishnu pondered. "Love, the force that binds us, the very essence of our being. How can it be preserved in the face of such immense dissolution?"

Lakshmi leaned closer, her eyes reflecting a thousand celestial stars. "Our love, my love," she said, her voice filled with conviction, "is woven into the very fabric of the cosmos. It is present in every act of creation, it sustains every being in existence, and it will continue to inspire long after this kalpa fades into nothingness."

VISHNU PONDERED LAKSHMI'S words, a flicker of hope igniting within him. He understood the essence of her message – their love, a cosmic force, couldn't be obliterated by the Pralaya. But the concern of his avatars, the ones who would carry the burden of preservation, remained. How could they be imbued with the knowledge, not just of his duties, but also of the love that fueled his resolve?

Lost in thought, Vishnu closed his eyes, his mind traversing the vast expanse of the cosmos. He delved into the celestial archives, a repository of knowledge accumulated across eons. He sought an answer, a solution that would bridge the gap between kalpas, ensuring that the lessons learned and the love that guided him would be passed on to his future selves.

Suddenly, a vision unfolded before him. He saw a celestial lotus, its petals shimmering with an otherworldly glow. Unlike the lotus from which Lakshmi had emerged, this one held a different purpose. It wasn't a vessel for creation; it was a vessel for remembrance.

Within the lotus, Vishnu envisioned a condensed form of their experiences – their shared victories, their moments of tenderness, the unwavering devotion that bound them together. It would be a repository of their love story, a beacon that would guide his future avatars, reminding them of the purpose that fueled their existence.

Opening his eyes, a resolute expression settled on his face. He turned to Lakshmi, his voice filled with newfound determination. "My love," he said, "I have found the answer. We shall create a seed of remembrance, a celestial lotus that will carry the essence of our love and our experiences across the kalpas."

Lakshmi's face lit up with a radiant smile. "A beautiful idea, my love," she said, her voice brimming with excitement. "This seed will ensure that even amidst the darkness, the light of our love will shine through, guiding your avatars and reminding them of their purpose."

Together, Vishnu and Lakshmi began the process of creating the celestial lotus. They infused it with their combined energies, weaving their experiences, their love, and their unwavering commitment to the preservation of the cosmos into its very essence. As they poured their love into the lotus, it pulsed with a radiant light, a testament to the power they were channeling.

Finally, the celestial lotus bloomed, its petals shimmering with a brilliance that rivaled a thousand suns. Within its heart, a single seed lay nestled, a tiny vessel brimming with the essence of their love story. This seed, Vishnu declared, would be entrusted to the care of Narada, the celestial sage and chronicler of time.

Narada, renowned for his wisdom and unwavering devotion to the divine, readily accepted the responsibility. He understood the immense significance of the seed, the bridge it would create between kalpas. He vowed to safeguard it until the time came for it to fulfill its purpose.

With the seed of remembrance safely entrusted to Narada, a sense of peace settled upon Vishnu and Lakshmi. They knew that even in the face of the inevitable Pralaya, their love story would not be lost. It would live on, a guiding light for his future avatars, a testament to the enduring power of love that bound them together and safeguarded the cosmos.

Eons passed, measured not by the ticking of clocks but by the grand cycles of creation and destruction. The universe pulsed with life, then plunged into darkness, a cosmic dance that had no beginning and no end. Vishnu, the preserver, manifested in various forms – Rama, the righteous prince; Krishna, the playful charioteer; and countless others. Each avatar embodied the essence of Vishnu, upholding dharma (righteousness) and restoring balance to the cosmos.

However, the memories of past kalpas faded with each creation. The avatars, though imbued with the principles of preservation, lacked the knowledge of the specific challenges they might face or the inspiration drawn from past victories. It was here that the seed of remembrance played its crucial role.

One such instance occurred during the Ramayana, the epic tale of Rama, Vishnu's seventh avatar. Rama, along with his loyal wife Sita and his brother Lakshmana, faced a seemingly insurmountable challenge – the abduction of Sita by the demon king Ravana. As despair threatened to engulf them, a faint memory flickered within Rama's consciousness.

It was a fragmented vision, a glimpse of a celestial lotus pulsating with an ethereal light. He saw a figure, his own yet different, standing beside a woman of radiant beauty. Though the details remained elusive, a sense of overwhelming love and unwavering resolve washed over him. In that instant, Rama understood. He was not alone in this battle; he was guided by the legacy of countless battles fought and victories won in kalpas past.

The memory, though fleeting, rekindled Rama's determination. He knew, with unwavering certainty, that he had to rescue Sita, not just for his personal happiness but to uphold the principles of dharma. This echo of love, a fragment of the seed of remembrance, served as a beacon in his darkest hour, reminding him of his purpose and the strength that resided within him.

Similar echoes resonated within other avatars of Vishnu. Krishna, during the Kurukshetra war, felt a surge of courage as he faced the Kaurava army. Within him, a faint memory flickered – a vision of two figures standing hand-in-hand, their combined energies radiating an aura of unwavering support. Though he couldn't decipher the memory fully, he understood its essence – the power of unity and the unwavering support that fueled his resolve.

These echoes of love, whispers from across kalpas, played a vital role in shaping the actions of Vishnu's avatars. They instilled within them the courage to face adversity, the wisdom to navigate complex situations, and the unwavering commitment to uphold dharma. Though the complete story of their love remained a mystery, its essence resonated throughout the ages, a testament to the enduring power of Vishnu and Lakshmi's bond.

The seed of remembrance, entrusted to Narada, remained a silent but potent force. It served as a bridge between kalpas, ensuring that the legacy of Vishnu and Lakshmi's love story continued to inspire, guide, and empower his avatars in their eternal quest to preserve the cosmos.

The Pralaya, the great dissolution, finally arrived. The universe, once a vibrant tapestry of life, succumbed to the inevitable. Stars collapsed, galaxies imploded, and existence dissolved into a primordial singularity. Even the divine abodes, including Vaikuntha, were not spared. Vishnu and Lakshmi, their forms dissolving into the cosmic soup, embraced each other one last time.

Yet, amidst the all-encompassing darkness, a flicker of light remained. The seed of remembrance, nestled within the care of Narada, remained untouched by the forces of destruction. It pulsed with a faint luminescence, a tiny ember holding onto the essence of their love story and the wisdom it contained.

As eons passed, a new creation stirred within the void. Slowly, a new universe began to take shape. Galaxies coalesced, stars ignited, and the seeds of life were sown on nascent planets. Narada, the lone survivor of the Pralaya, his celestial form shimmering with an otherworldly glow, emerged into this nascent universe.

His primary mission remained unchanged – to safeguard the seed of remembrance until the time came for Vishnu's next avatar to emerge. He watched over the fledgling universe, a silent observer as life took root and flourished on countless worlds.

Finally, the moment arrived. A new consciousness, imbued with the essence of Vishnu, began to stir within a mortal realm. This was the beginning of Vishnu's next avatar, a new chapter in the grand narrative of preservation.

As the avatar's consciousness fully formed, a faint echo from across the kalpas resonated within him. It was a memory, fragmented yet powerful, of a celestial lotus pulsating with an ethereal light. He saw two figures, one radiating strength and serenity, the other embodying grace and compassion. Though the details remained elusive, a wave of love and unwavering resolve washed over him.

This echo, a whisper from the seed of remembrance planted by Vishnu and Lakshmi eons ago, served as his awakening. He understood his purpose – to uphold dharma, to restore balance, and to carry forward the legacy of the love story that had shaped countless kalpas.

With newfound determination, the avatar embarked on his journey. He faced challenges, overcame obstacles, and upheld the principles of righteousness with unwavering resolve. Though he may not have possessed the complete memory of Vishnu and Lakshmi's love story, the echo it left within him served as a guiding light, a testament to the enduring power of love that bound the cosmos together.

And so, the cycle continued. Vishnu, through his avatars, would forever safeguard the universe, while the seed of remembrance, a beacon of their love story, would bridge the gap between kalpas, ensuring that the legacy of love, preservation, and harmony would forever resonate within the ever-evolving cosmos.

About the Author

Mrigendra Bharti, born on June 29, 2004, in South Delhi, India, is a multifaceted individual recognized as the owner of Mrigendra Bharti Group InfoTech India Co. Pvt Ltd. Beyond his entrepreneurial endeavors, he is a distinguished music producer, director, and a budding writer.

Embarking on his professional journey at a young age, Mrigendra Bharti's visionary leadership has led to the establishment of several successful ventures, including Croma Music Series Entertainment, Sellbrochure, Fauget Innovative, and more.

What sets Mrigendra apart is his early initiation into the world of business. His foray into the unknown realms of entrepreneurship began during his 10th-grade years, where he delved into the music industry. This initial venture laid the foundation for subsequent achievements, showcasing his dedication and resilience.

Having honed his skills in music, Mrigendra Bharti not only demonstrated significant growth in his craft but also expanded his professional network. His passion extends beyond music, encompassing app and website development, as well as graphic design.

Fueled by his creative aspirations, Mrigendra established the Mrigendra Bharti Group, a company specializing in website and app development. Currently, he collaborates with a dedicated team, collectively working on ambitious projects that promise innovation and excellence.

Mrigendra's journey serves as an inspiration, particularly for today's students, highlighting the potential of youthful determination and the ability to transform innovative ideas into successful businesses. As he continues to make strides in various domains, Mrigendra Bharti remains a dynamic force, contributing vibrancy to the realms of business, music, and technology.

Read more at https://www.imwriter-mrigendra.rf.gd.